THE ELECTRIC BOOK

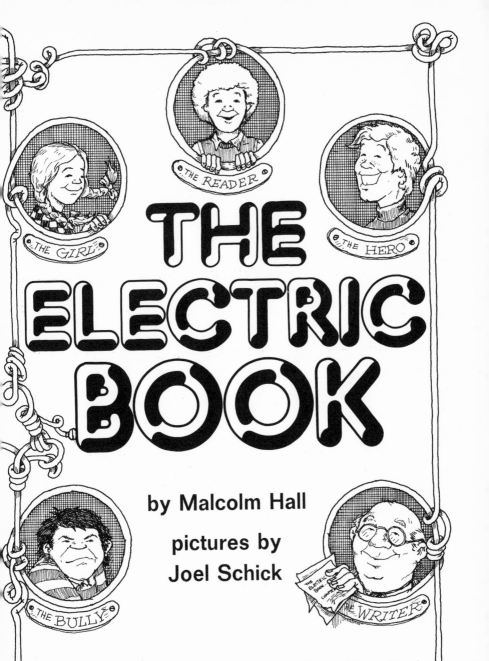

THE ELECTRIC BOOK

THE READER

THE GIRL

THE HERO

THE BULLY

THE WRITER

by Malcolm Hall

pictures by
Joel Schick

Coward, McCann & Geoghegan, Inc. New York

SBN: GB-698-30592-2
SBN: TR-698-20339-9
Library of Congress Catalog Card Number: 75-10454

Printed in the United States of America

10216

For Mary

THE
ELECTRIC
BOOK

CHAPTER ONE

Martin, as usual, stood at the very end of the line. He enjoyed being there, especially on field trips. Martin wasn't shy, but he liked the fact that his teacher, Mr. Gunderson, hardly ever noticed him behind all the other students. That meant Martin was able to see more of the really interesting things without being constantly told to pay attention.

Martin's class was touring a company called Unlimited Electronics, Incorporated. The company made electrical appliances and gadgets of all kinds. So far, the tour was a bore.

The morning had begun with Mr. J. J. Jay, the president of the company. Mr. Jay had told the class how great he and his company were. Then a publicity director, Mrs. Harper, marched the class off, leading it up one hallway and down another.

Martin had seen nothing but crates of light bulbs and rows of electric can openers. As far as he was concerned, he might as well have been going through a department store.

Now Mrs. Harper had stopped again. She opened a door and invited the class to look inside. "This room is especially interesting," she said. "This is where we make electric sewing machines."

Martin groaned and looked away. What did he care about hitches and stitches? He had come hoping to see *inventions*, new machines that did things differently. And, even more, Martin wanted to meet some real inventors.

He imagined the inventors would have long white beards. They would wear long white coats. Being so absent-minded, they would stir their coffee with slide rules and then forget to drink it. Martin planned to be an inventor someday. He practiced being absent-minded by skipping breakfast.

But as Martin groaned and looked away, he noticed a door a little way down the hall. On the outside of the door were the words: NEW PRODUCT RESEARCH AND DEVELOPMENT. EXTREMELY PRIVATE. KEEP THIS DOOR CLOSED AT ALL TIMES. THIS MEANS YOU! The door was halfway open.

It had to be where the inventors worked! Luckily, Martin was wearing his sneakers. He took a quick and quiet step backward, keeping his eyes all the while on the lecturing lady.

The other students were busy listening to Mrs. Harper trying to explain what happens when the big needle with the thread goes down through the cloth. Even Mr. Gunderson seemed to be having trouble understanding how sewing machines work.

Martin took a second step, and then another. He reached out behind and touched a corner where the hallway made a turn to the right. Martin took a deep breath, then ducked around the corner. He was just in time. Mrs. Harper had finished her talk.

The whole class, whispering and shuffling the way they weren't supposed to, went off down the hall. They filed through a pair of swinging double doors and disappeared from sight.

Martin knew he could catch up with the class

later. The bus taking them back to school left at one o'clock. Martin had a whole hour. And all he wanted to do was have a quick look inside the room with the forbidding sign and the partly opened door.

He tiptoed across the hallway and looked in.

And there was Mr. J. J. Jay! He was still bragging, this time to two men and a woman. His words weren't very clear, though. They all seemed to be about "plots" and "chapters."

So the room wasn't for inventors after all. Too bad. Martin turned to walk away. Then he heard, clear as a bell, Mr. Jay speak the words: "But I've been talking too much. Let's have a look at my fantastic new invention."

Martin's ears perked up. He hurried back to the door for another look. This time he opened the door a bit wider and stuck his head partway into the room. Then he gasped with amazement.

In the very middle of the room stood a huge metal cube, with sides of polished steel. Orange and green lights flashed like the eyes of winking robots. Wavy lines chased themselves across oscilloscope screens. Needles jumped back and forth on gauges, and a hum of electricity filled the air. Now *that* was an invention!

Mr. Jay rapped on the box with his knuckles.

"The Reader goes in here," he said.

"And then what happens, J.J.?" asked the woman. Of the three listeners, she seemed to have the most interest in the invention. The other two appeared to be a little afraid of the machine and were whispering nervously to each other.

"That's a very good question, Fredrika," said Mr. Jay. "After the Reader goes into the Electric Book, the Writer begins the story."

"And then what happens?" asked Fredrika again.

J.J. frowned. "That's only a so-so question. I'm not quite sure yet. I suppose the Reader meets the characters."

"How exciting!" Fredrika clapped her hands. "And what happens next?"

"That's a terrible question!" shouted J.J. "I don't know. I haven't read the Book."

This startled everyone. "You haven't?" the three listeners said together.

"Of course not," said J.J. "That's why I've asked you three vice-presidents here. I need a volunteer to be the first Reader."

The vice-presidents gulped and looked as if they wished they were somewhere else. "Ordinarily," said one of the men, "I'd be glad to try out a new invention. But I never read a book, electric or otherwise, unless I know something about it first. Otherwise, how could I know if the book is good or bad?"

"Have you ever tried making up your own mind?" asked J.J. sarcastically.

"Well, of course, I have," the man explained. "And I made up my mind that someone else has got to tell me what to think. That's my decision, and I'm going to stick to it!"

Mr. Jay sighed and looked at the other man. "If Bob doesn't want to try the Book, how about you, Cal?"

Cal blushed and looked down at this feet. "I've never been too much for reading, J.J. The long words always threw me for a loop."

"Oh, come on," said J.J. in exasperation. "I told you all just a minute ago that there *aren't* any words in the Electric Book. It reads by itself. That's why I invented the Book in the first place. To make reading *easy*."

Fredrika shook her head. "J.J., Clarence and Bob are trying to tell you that they're afraid to try out your invention. Frankly, I am too. It looks dangerous."

"Balderdash," scoffed J.J. "Why, it's perfectly safe. That machine is no more dangerous than any of my other inventions."

"That's just the point!" said Clarence. "Remember the Electric Shoelacer you made me try? My toes still hurt when I think about it!"

"Yeah, and what about the Electric Basketball you invented?" added Bob indignantly. "One bounce and it sent *me* flying into the basket. Never again!"

"Okay! Okay! I admit some of my ideas haven't worked out, but this one is different. The Electric Book will work. I *know* it will. If I only had a Reader, I'd prove it. But what happens? Everybody is afraid!"

"I'm not."

"Who said that?" shouted J.J. All heads turned toward the laboratory door.

Martin stepped into the room. "I did. I'll try out your Book."

CHAPTER TWO

"Bravo!" shouted J.J. "What an act of cour-age!" He ran over to Martin and practically dragged him back to the Electric Book, all the while explaining the hows and whys of the machine. Mr. Jay finished by saying, "So once you're inside the Book, you have nothing to do but sit back and enjoy the story."

"Suppose I don't like the story?" asked Mar-tin. "Is there any way for me to stop it?"

"Why of course!" said J.J. "What sort of book

would it be if the Reader couldn't quit any time he wanted?"

Mr. Jay pulled open a drawer on one side of the machine and took out a black leather belt with a large, solid silver buckle. In the center of the buckle, there was a red button. Mr. Jay gave the belt to Martin.

"Keep this belt with you at all times. If you want to get out of the Book, just push the button. With an old-fashioned book, the Reader says 'ugh' by closing the pages. This Book is modern, so you'll need a switch."

As Martin strapped the belt around his waist, Mr. Jay busied himself by twisting dials and turning knobs on the machine to get it ready. The machine began to hum ominously, and for the first time Martin felt a little nervous.

Martin was not the only one to be nervous. Clarence, too, had a worried look on his face. He knelt beside Martin and said, "Son, I'd like to give you a little warning."

"Ah-ah-ah," said Mr. Jay hastily. "Let him read the Book first. You can warn him later."

"Now what good will that do, J.J.?"

"None at all," muttered J.J. merrily. He took Martin by the arm and led him up to the machine. He opened the door. "Just step in here, Martin."

Martin felt himself being pushed, from behind, into the Book. Suddenly, Clarence shouted, "Don't trust the Book! Don't trust any of J.J.'s inventions!"

But then the door closed, leaving Martin alone.

It was pitch dark inside the machine. The only sound was the low eerie hum of machinery. Then even the hum stopped.

Suddenly a sign made of small bright red lights flashed inside the tiny room. The sign said: CHAPTER TWO. The story had begun!

But that can't be right! Martin thought. What had happened to Chapter One? Already the Book was going haywire. He decided to tell Mr. Jay before anything else went wrong.

Martin felt in the dark for the door handle. When he found it, he gave a sharp yank. The door swung open, and Martin stepped outside the machine.

Right onto a wide, empty grassy field. The laboratory, Mr. Jay, and the vice-presidents were nowhere in sight.

Martin turned around and around. All he could see were green, rolling hills and a few clouds in the distance. Then he realized he had turned a complete circle. The Electric Book was gone, too.

So this is automatic reading, thought Martin.

He spotted a road about twenty feet in front of him. If something were going to happen, it would probably be along the road. Martin walked over to the road and sat down beside it.

Whatever was going to happen, Martin hoped it would hurry up. Since he had to be back in an hour, there wasn't much time to waste. Also, Martin liked his books to have plenty of action in them.

Just at that moment, a station wagon came over the top of a nearby hill, speeding along at eighty. As the car shot by, the driver glanced at Martin. The driver's mouth fell open with surprise.

And with that, the car's brakes slammed on with a screech! The station wagon fishtailed and skidded to a stop about a quarter of a mile down the road. Then, with a clunk and a rattle, the driver put his car in reverse and backed up the road until he was again even with Martin.

The driver, a kindly looking man with wire-rimmed glasses and a baseball cap, leaned across the front seat and rolled down the window. "Hop in, son," said the man cheerfully.

Martin smiled back, but shook his head. "No thanks." He had been told again and again never to accept rides from strangers.

The man looked surprised and even a little angry. "What are you trying to do, slow us down? The game should have started by now."

"What game?" asked Martin. "And who is this 'us' you say I'm slowing down?"

"Us! The team!" And the driver pointed to the back of the station wagon. There was no one at all inside.

The driver groaned and slapped his forehead. "Blast!" he shouted. "Forgot 'em completely. Hold your horses. I'll be back in a second."

The man stepped on the gas. Still in reverse, the station wagon shot backward over the hill.

Martin watched all this in amazement. What in the world was going on? It certainly wasn't like any book he had ever read before.

Then the car reappeared. Again it screeched to a stop beside Martin. But this time the back of the station wagon was filled with children. They were all about Martin's age and wore baseball uniforms.

The driver rolled down the window exactly as he had before. "Hop in, son," he said cheerfully.

Martin was about to say no again, since he really didn't see what difference it made that other kids were in the car. Then he realized there was only one explanation. This was part of the story! If he didn't get into the car, nothing could happen. Anyway, as long as he was

only in a story, he should be safe—or so he thought.

Martin said, "Thanks," and slid into the front seat. The driver started up his car again and drove off.

"By the way," said the driver, "Why don't you meet the team? Team, introduce yourselves."

Martin looked into the back of the station wagon. A boy with sandy blond hair and freckles smiled widely. "Hi, I'm Bob, the Hero."

Another boy tried to smile, but couldn't. He had dark, angry eyes and a face so mean no smile could ever come out. "My name's Spike," he said sullenly. "I'm the Bully."

Between the two boys was a girl who was also wearing a baseball uniform. She wore her hair in braids and seemed to be the type who wrinkled her nose and laughed a lot. "I'm Becky," she said. "The Girl."

"Girl!" exclaimed Martin. "What's a Girl doing in a baseball story?"

Becky's eyes flashed angrily. "What's *wrong* with a Girl in a baseball story?" She doubled up her fist and held it under Martin's nose.

"Nothing!" said Martin very quickly. "Nothing at all."

"Now, team," said the driver, "let's not argue. And by the way, Becky, you mean a baseball *team*, not a story, don't you? This is real life, *remember?*"

"Oh, sure." Becky giggled. Then she whispered to Spike, "The Writer's mad because his Book started out so badly. Imagine, skipping the whole first chapter and starting out in Chapter Two!"

"What gets me," whispered Spike, "is the way he forgot *us*, too." Then they both laughed out loud although Spike's laugh was more like a snarl.

"Hey!" shouted the driver. "What's going on back there?"

At this, Bob, who had been eavesdropping on Becky and Spike, spoke up in a sing-songy voice. "It's Becky and Spike. They're laughing at you behind your back, Mr. Writ—"

"Tattletale!" shouted Becky, and she clapped her hand over Bob's mouth.

"MMMPH!" was all Bob could say.

Martin turned to the driver. "Is that true? Are you really the Writer of this Book?"

The driver slunk down in his seat and looked warily at Martin from the corner of his eye. "What if I am?"

"Because if you are," said Martin, "I'd like to find out a few things. For instance, when is anything interesting going to happen? And when—"

The driver desperately reached for a switch on the car's dashboard. "Right now," he said, as he flipped the switch. "We're just in time for The Game!"

CHAPTER THREE

Martin blinked. Something very odd had happened. Looking back on it later, he would say, very calmly, "Then the scene shifted." But for now he was speechless.

The road, the car, even the hills—everything had disappeared. Martin was still sitting, but now he was on a wooden bench worn smooth from many sittings. Behind him were bleachers filled with laughing and cheering spectators. Boys selling peanuts and cold pop walked up and down the aisles of the stands. In front was a fenced-in field. The team with which Martin had ridden was out in the field doing toe-touches and push-ups. He was in a baseball park!

Way out in center field stood a scoreboard covered with flashing, winking lights. The lights spelled out messages, like WELCOME SLUGS and BUY POPCORN. Suddenly the lights flashed CHAPTER THREE, and then they went on to something else.

The chapter sign reminded Martin of the Book. He looked around the park. Martin was sure now the driver was the Writer, and that flipping the switch had changed chapters. But the driver was nowhere to be seen.

Instead, an Umpire, wearing a thick, barred mask, like the ones worn by catchers, strolled up to home plate and dusted it off. Then the Umpire stood up and shouted, "Play ball!" It was the start of the strangest game Martin had ever seen.

Martin's team, or at least the one he had arrived with, was named the Flyers. The other team called themselves the Slugs.

While the Flyers (except for Spike) all looked honest and reasonably friendly, the Slugs, player for player, seemed as evil as any gangster. Some had thick, handlebar mustaches, though the players were only ten years old! Not a minute went by that one member of the

Slugs didn't chase a dog, insult a fan, or do something else just as obnoxious.

Oh, come on, thought Martin. *I know in books the visiting team is supposed to be bad, but this is ridiculous.*

The game was even more unbelievable.

In the first inning, Becky singled. Then she stole second base. And then she stole third! The Flyers still had no outs. Everyone in the stands cheered wildly. Even Martin was getting excited.

The Slugs' pitcher threw a high hard pitch to the batter. It was another ball. Just as the catcher threw the ball back to the pitcher, Becky broke, running for home! The fans jumped to their feet.

The Slugs' pitcher caught the ball. For a split second he froze, trying to decide whether to tag Becky himself or throw the ball back to the catcher. Then he threw.

Dust exploded in a cloud as Becky slid into home plate, just before the ball arrived. The Umpire leaned over the base, then spread his arms wide. "Safe!"

Everyone roared. The first run, and Becky had done it all herself! The score was 1–0, and there were still no outs.

But then, without any warning, the game jumped into the fourth inning! Martin couldn't believe his eyes. Now Spike was pitching and the Slugs were batting.

The first Slug hit a double; the next one slammed a triple off the right-field wall. That was followed by a single, and so on, until four runs had scored. There was still only one out, when the teams started to change sides once more!

That was too much for Martin. He jumped off the bench and ran out onto the field.

"What's happening?" he shouted at the Umpire. "What happened to the rest of the first inning? For that matter, what happened to the second and the third inning? Only one out's been made in the whole game!"

The Umpire looked insulted. "What's wrong with that?" he asked. "The fans are cheering. Listen to them. They came to see action, not a lot of outs."

"But it's not the way the game is played," insisted Martin.

The Umpire glanced to one side and then the other. He lowered his voice, and said, "Look, I really shouldn't explain, but since you're new, I will. In the Book, it says 'Nothing happened after Becky stole home until the fourth inning.' We just finished with the fourth inning. Now we're going to the bottom of the ninth."

Martin was stunned. "The bottom of the ninth! What about the fifth, sixth—"

"Nothing exciting happens, so we don't *need* them!" snapped the Umpire. "They're not in the Book." And he turned his back and dusted off the plate again.

Martin glared at the Umpire. He remembered his belt and thought about turning off the Book right then and there. But he did sort of want to see how everything came out, so he walked back to the bench.

And so it was the ninth inning. The Umpire had said so, the scoreboard said so, and the fans seemed to be happy. They cheered everything, no matter what.

It was the Flyers' turn to bat. The score was four to one, favor of the Slugs. For some reason, the Flyers had started the inning with two men out and the bases loaded. All at once the fans began cheering louder than ever.

"A good hitter must be coming up," said Martin out loud.

"Right you are," said a voice beside him.

Martin turned. It was Becky, who had walked over from the Flyer dugout. For once, she was not laughing. Instead she looked bored.

"Who is it, anyhow?" asked Martin. The batter still hadn't reached the plate.

"It's Bob the Hero, of course." Becky sighed. She closed her eyes and yawned.

"Hey, you're right!" Martin pointed. "There

33

he is. He's in the batter's box. Aren't you even going to look? This is your team's last chance."

"Uh-huh," murmured Becky. She was busy balancing a bat on the tips of her fingers.

"STRIKE ONE!" shouted the Umpire.

"Do you hear that? He's only got two strikes left!"

"I know," answered Becky. Daintily, she tipped over and stood on her head.

"STRIKE TWO!"

"Becky! Bob's going to strike out. Aren't you worried?"

"Not a bit." As she said this, Becky did a back flip and landed on her feet facing Martin.

"CRAK!" came the sound of a bat hitting a ball. There was a huge cheer, the loudest of the day. An excited voice came over the loud-speaker. "Look at that, fans! It's going, going, gone! The Flyers win—five to four!"

"See?" said Becky. "The good guys win again."

Martin stood up and looked around uncertainly. "Is that the end of the Book?"

The bored look on Becky's face went away and the mischievous smile came back. "A lot more happens," she said. "Look over there."

Martin looked. In front of the home dugout, Spike and Bob had faced off, ready to fight. Both were plainly angry and had their fists up.

As Martin hurried over, he could hear Bob boasting, "See Spike, I did it again. I hit a home run to win the game. You almost made us lose with your terrible pitching. I'm the star and you're a bum!"

"Hey, Bob," said Martin suddenly, "you shouldn't be mad. The Flyers still won the—"

"Who asked you?" sneered Bob, and he gave Martin a shove.

"Leave him alone!" ordered Spike. "The Reader hasn't done anything to you."

"Maybe not," snarled Bob. "But I'm sure going to do something to *you*. You know what the Writer planned. At the end of Chapter Three the Hero and the Bully fight, and the Hero wins. Well, I'm the Hero, and you're the Bully, so put 'em up!"

And then the two boys were swinging wildly at each other. Even though Spike was bigger than Bob, it was obvious to Martin that Bob would win. Heroes always beat Bullies in books. He had to break up the fight!

Just at that moment, the Umpire walked past. He paid no attention to the brawl. The Umpire's face mask was off, and for the first time Martin could see him clearly. He was wearing a thick pair of wire-rimmed glasses.

It was the Writer!

Martin rushed up and grabbed the man's

arm. "Can't you stop the fight? The wrong person's winning. Bob should be the Bully, not the Hero!"

The Writer simply shrugged his shoulders. "Too bad," he said calmly. "That's the way I wrote it, and that's the way it stays. It's too much trouble to write things over."

"Well, I've got news for you," said Martin angrily. "I never did like baseball stories much, and I really don't like this one. I'm going to turn off this Book right now, and I'm going to tell Mr. Jay what I think of it!"

As Martin said these words, he was reaching for the button on the belt.

"Oh no," shouted the Writer, "*anything* but that." Then he pointed up in the air behind Martin's head. "Watch out!"

Martin started to turn. But he didn't turn fast enough. A pop bottle, added to the story at the last moment by the Writer, flew out of the stands and hit Martin square on the head.

"UHHH!" he grunted, and fell over.

The Writer looked down at Martin. He decided it was just as good a place as any to end the chapter. So he did.

CHAPTER FOUR

"I don't care what you say, Bob. I still think it's a dirty trick to play on anybody. Even a Reader." Becky, Bob, and Spike were sitting around Martin, who was still sleeping peacefully.

"And I say, Becky, that it serves him right," sneered Bob. "He wrecked the baseball story completely. I just wish the Writer hadn't put us here along with him."

The three glanced around forlornly. They

were perched on a tiny log raft no larger than a car. All around the raft danced the waves of the Atlantic Ocean.

"Anyway," Bob continued, "I sure was good, wasn't I? Did you see my home run, Becky?"

"I honestly didn't bother," Becky snapped. "If I've read it once, I've read it a million times."

Bob paid no attention. "And that fight! Wow! What a battle!"

"Oh, yeah?" said Spike. "It's easy to win when it's part of the story. How'd you like to try again out here?"

Bob backed up to the edge of the raft. "Now see here, Spike. The Writer didn't say anything about a fight in *this* chapter, and anyway. . . ."

"SHHH!" whispered Becky suddenly. "The Reader's waking up."

Martin groaned and opened his eyes. His head hurt, and his back was stiff and sore. Where was he? He couldn't be at home, not with all that sky overhead. And what was he lying on? For that matter, why was he rocking back and forth?

Martin rolled over on his side, looked, and groaned even louder. Then he saw Bob, who still looked a little hazy.

"Where are we?" said Martin slowly. "And where did all the water come from?"

"Those are the dancing waves of the Atlantic Ocean, if I remember correctly," said Bob. "At least, I think that's how the Writer wrote it."

Becky touched Martin's shoulder. "Don't let him confuse you. I'm Becky, the Girl, remember? And this is Spike, the Bully." Spike nodded, trying to look as pleasant as possible. But it was hard with his Bully's face.

"And I'm sure you remember *me*," said Bob. "I'm Bob, the Hero, the one who—"

"Was such a brat!" exclaimed Martin. He sat up. "I get it now. I'm still in the Book. But how did we get here?"

Spike tried to explain. "When you tried to stop the Book, the Writer got scared. So he switched everything around. We're in a new Chapter. Even the *story* is different."

"Right," broke in Bob. "Now, this story is about four kids marooned on an uncharted island. In the last Chapter, our ship went down. In this Chapter, we spot the shore. In the next Chapter, we reach land. That's one day from now."

"One day!" exclaimed Martin.

"That's right. But don't worry, we've already been here two days."

"Two days!"

Bob nodded. "But you were lucky and slept through them. Anyway, once we get to the island it's eighteen years before we're rescued."

"Eighteen *years!*" shouted Martin.

Bob looked worried. He dropped his voice and whispered, "You'd better stop repeating everything I say. The Writer doesn't think it sounds very good."

"I don't care what the Writer thinks!" Martin screamed. "I can't spend eighteen years inside a book." Martin threw up his hands. "What am I saying? I shouldn't have spent even a day! My parents will kill me. Mr. Gunderson will fail me. I don't care *what* it does to you Characters, I'm turning off this Book."

Martin reached for his belt. Then he gasped. "It's gone! My belt is gone!"

"We know." Becky nodded sadly. "The Writer stole it between Chapters." Becky glanced at Spike and Bob. She had a questioning look on her face. Spike and Bob nodded at her.

Becky turned back to Martin. "I know you're worried," she said. "And we feel bad about what the Writer's done. While you were sleeping, Bob, Spike, and I talked it over. We've decided to help you get the belt back."

Martin looked up gratefully. "That's super. But why? I mean, you work for the Writer, don't you?"

"Only because we have to," said Becky bitterly. "We don't like him at all. The Writer can make us do anything, say anything, *be* anything he wants. Do you think Spike likes being a Bully? Or that I like having to laugh all the time?"

"It's even worse than that," complained Spike. "If the Writer decided to, he could get rid of any of us Characters just like that!" Spike snapped his fingers. "All the Writer would have to do is write, 'Then Spike fell overboard and was never seen again.' And that would be the end of *me*."

Martin shook his head. "That is bad." Then he frowned. "But if the Writer can do all that, what chance do *we* have?"

It was Becky's turn again. "For one thing, he can't get rid of *you*. You're the Reader. Without you, the Book stops. For another thing, we know most of the Writer's tricks. Together, we just might be able to outwit him."

Martin thought for a moment. Then he said, "It's a deal," and he stuck out his hand.

The four put their hands together and shook them. For the next ten minutes or so, they talked feverishly until finally they decided on a plan. It wasn't a very good plan, but it was the only one they had, so it would have to be used.

The idea was simple. The first step was to slow down the raft. If the raft didn't land on the island as it was supposed to, the Writer would have to intervene and change his story again. The more times the Writer changed his story, the better chance Martin, Becky, Spike, and Bob would have to catch him.

Martin and Becky knelt on one side of the raft, while Spike and Bob got down on the other. At a signal from Becky, the four dipped their hands in the ocean and began to paddle.

It was slow going at first, but soon the raft stopped drifting. The current pushed one way, and the rowers pulled the other.

"Now what?" panted Martin.

"Something will happen, you'll see," Becky gasped. "We've stopped the story. The Writer will have to do something to get the action going again."

"I sure hope he does it soon—hey! Watch out!" Martin, who had been gazing into the ocean as he rowed, had caught a glimpse of something long and dark rising rapidly from the bottom of the sea. He spun around and grabbed Becky, pulling her arm out of the water.

Just as he did, the water beside the raft exploded in spray. "Shark!"

Two rows of needle-sharp teeth snapped shut. The smooth gray fish with its little pig eyes rolled past the raft. Its high back fin sliced the water. The shark was twice as long as the raft.

Swimming just below the surface, the shark continued on for twenty feet or so, then made a long lazy circle. The fish was getting ready for another pass.

"Everyone to the middle of the raft!" shouted Martin. The four huddled together, making extra sure some stray arm or leg was not within reach. "Here it comes again."

The shark swam lazily, almost peacefully. If Martin hadn't seen its teeth, he might not even have been afraid. But he realized how quickly one snap could have removed Becky's hand.

The fish seemed unable to make up its mind about what to do. It nudged the raft once from underneath with its nose. Then it bumped the logs a little harder, but with its bony head this time.

This seemed to give the shark an idea, for it swam off a short distance and then turned around once more. The meaning was clear.

"Look out!" shouted Martin. "It's going to ram us."

With two short, strong sweeps of its tail, the

shark came rushing in. Just before it hit, it ducked slightly, so as to come up under the raft and turn it over.

There was a loud, crunching sound. The raft folded up in the middle and jumped out of the water. Martin felt himself rising, turning, and then falling.

The moment before Martin hit the water, he managed to take a deep breath. He came up splashing. He quickly shook the saltwater out of his eyes and looked around. Spike, Becky, and Bob were scattered on all sides of the raft. They were treading water, though, and seemed to be all right.

Martin raised one arm and waved. "Get back on the raft before the shark circles back," he shouted.

Martin swam for the raft, but without much hope. The ocean was not like a swimming pool. Waves kept breaking over him, and he felt as though he were not moving at all. His arms stroked and his feet kicked, but he wasn't getting any closer to the raft.

Because the raft was moving too! Martin hadn't been sure at first, but now he was positive. And it wasn't moving in a straight line, either, but was circling, stopping, backing up, and then circling again. Suddenly the raft turned and headed right toward Martin.

That's handy, he thought at first. Then a second, horrible thought came. Martin ducked his head under the water and opened his eyes quickly, just for a second. It was time enough to see that the shark was under the raft and was coming after him.

Martin turned and started to swim away. But he knew it was hopeless. Who could out-swim a shark?

"Martin! Martin!" The shouts came from behind him. Martin kept swimming, but his strokes were turning into splashes. In another minute he would be too tired to move.

"Get on the raft!" It was Becky. Martin looked back over his shoulder wearily. The raft was closing in fast. But now Becky, Spike, and Bob were standing on top of it. They were waving frantically.

Becky put both hands to her mouth. "Don't worry about the shark. "It can't get to you!"

Martin didn't understand and didn't care either. He was too tired to do anything.

The logs came closer and closer. He could see the shark's head. Its mouth was open, ready for the kill. But the shark never reached Martin. It couldn't.

Becky had already pulled Martin onto the raft before he realized the truth. The shark's back fin had slipped between the logs and was jammed tight. The shark was stuck beneath the raft, and its head couldn't reach beyond the edge.

Martin smiled weakly and sat down. "I thought you said I'd be *safe* in the Book." Then he sighed. "But we're still no closer to land."

"Not so!" shouted Bob. "Look where the shark is taking us!" He pointed to the horizon. In the distance were the skyscrapers of a large city.

"We'll get a ticker-tape parade." Becky giggled. "We'll *all* be Heroes."

"And we did it without the Writer's help," said Martin.

Spike turned around slowly when he heard this. "Are you kidding?" he said. "Who do you think sent the shark?"

CHAPTER FIVE

"I guess this is a new Chapter, huh?" asked Martin. He was sitting on a wooden floor, surrounded by wooden walls, and looking up at a wooden ceiling. "I thought we were going to have a ticker-tape parade and all that." Martin looked questioningly at Becky, Bob, and Spike, who were with him in the room, which was, more precisely, a shipping crate.

"Oh, but we did," said Bob. He tossed a newspaper into Martin's lap. The headlines read: **STURDY KIDS RESCUE PRINCE AT SEA**.

The article went on to say: "Famous child detectives were given a rousing ticker-tape welcome today following their daring rescue of Crown Prince Basil."

"*Basil?*" said Martin in disgust. "Who's Basil? Anyway, we all rescued ourselves, and I'm not a Prince."

Becky sighed. "In this Chapter you *are.* I'm afraid the Writer switched the story again. He was probably getting seasick."

Martin looked at the paper again. Beneath the headline he saw a photo of himself with three others. They were sitting on the back of a convertible, waving at a crowd while tons of confetti poured down from above.

"Why don't I remember any of that?" Martin asked after a moment.

"You're not expected to," said Becky. Plenty of things happen in books that the Characters don't know about. There just isn't enough room to put everything down. So the Writer makes it show up in a newspaper. Sometimes he just has us remember it."

"Even if it never really happened?"

"*Especially* if it never happened," said Becky triumphantly.

Martin shook his head. "I'm getting confused."

"Oh-oh," said Spike. "That's not good. Readers should *never* be confused. I'd better fill you in." Spike walked over to Martin and sat down beside him. Martin edged away a little.

"Relax," said Spike. "I'm not the Bully anymore. The Writer changed that too. Have you ever heard of the Sturdy Kids?"

"Sure, they were in the newspaper." Then Martin snapped his fingers. "I know! I've read all of their books. They're kid detectives who do everything in disguise. Don't tell me that you—"

Spike nodded. "We are indeed. And this is our Clubhouse. Don't you remember it from our books?"

Martin looked around the room. In the far corner away from him, he saw an old telephone. "I remember that! Your father, Roderick Sturdy, put that in for you. It happened in your second book, *The Case of the Busy Signal!*"

"Gee," said Bob, "you actually have read our books."

Martin looked at Bob and gasped. Between Chapters, Bob had gained about forty pounds! "You're Fat Bruce!" shouted Martin. "The Sturdy kid who always winds up the book by falling in a lake or sitting on a tack!"

Bob blushed. It was hard to be a Hero in one book and a Stooge in another.

Martin spun around and pointed at Becky.

"And your name in the Sturdy series is Gwen. Your hobby is making models and riding horses. There's a map of the world on the wall of your room and—who *are* you all, really?"

Becky smiled. "Why don't you keep on calling us Becky, Bob, and Spike? It'll be a lot simpler that way. Remember, we're still working *against* the Writer, not for him. That much is the same."

Martin nodded.

"And that reminds me," continued Becky, "I've found a clue."

"Isn't it funny about clues?" said Bob slyly. "They only happen in detective stories and nowhere else."

Becky ignored him. She casually held out a brass hotel key for Martin to look at. "I meant to show you this in the last Chapter, but after the shark showed up, I forgot. The Writer dropped it when he was stealing your belt."

Martin studied the plastic tag attached to the key. "It says 'Room 1313. The Deadwood Arms Hotel.' That sounds sinister."

"Not as sinister as a hotel I was once in," said Bob. "It was called the 'Wuldooya Inn'!"

For Spike, that was the last straw. "That's enough of your wisecracks, Bob. If you can't keep quiet, go outside and be a lookout."

"Aw, come on, Spike," began Bob. "The Writer made me say it." But Spike stamped his foot, and Bob scuttled out the door (which was a square hole covered with a Persian rug left over from a book the Writer had written about flying carpets).

"Where were we?" asked Spike.

"I was just thinking," said Becky. "If we're going to the Deadwood Arms, we'll need disguises. Since the Writer has already set Martin up as Prince Basil, maybe we should go as royalty, too."

"A fine idea," exclaimed Spike. He turned to Martin. "You stay here, while Becky and I get our costumes. We'll be back in a second." Becky and Spike then ducked out the back door, which was exactly like the front door, except that the rug had a different design.

Martin sat for a moment. Then he got up and went outside to talk to Bob. Martin felt sort of bad about the way Bob had been kicked out of the Clubhouse. If the Writer forced Bob to make wisecracks, how much of it was really Bob's fault?

But Bob wasn't there! Martin shrugged and went back inside the Clubhouse. *Maybe he needs a disguise too*, thought Martin.

Bob, however, was not going for a disguise. He was four blocks away by then, running as

hard as he could. According to the Writer's plan, he had just a few minutes before Spike and Becky would go back into the Clubhouse.

He ran past a gas station and into an empty parking lot. There Bob stopped and checked the street behind to make sure he had not been followed. Then he walked up to a large trash container, the kind that only trucks can haul away.

Bob knocked twice on the top.

"Password?" said a voice from within.

"You never said anything about a password!"

There was a pause. "Try again," said the voice.

"You never said *nothing* about a password!" said Bob triumphantly. "Right?"

"Right, except for the 'right'."

"Okay," said Bob in exasperation. "No 'right'."

"Fine, come in."

Bob lifted the top of the trash bin and climbed inside. Sitting in the very center and crouched over an old and very rusted typewriter was—the Writer!

"How's it going?" asked the Writer.

Bob winked. "Perfect. He swallowed the whole story."

The Writer polished his glasses with an old

leaf of lettuce and smiled. "He really thinks you're helping him, eh? You know, I hate to do it, in a way. Fool a Reader, that is. But what else am I going to do? If I don't fool him, he's bored. And if I do fool him, it's a trick!"

"Yeah, yeah," said Bob impatiently. "That's *your* problem, not mine. Just make sure you don't forget our deal. You know what you promised."

The Writer blinked in astonishment. "You weren't serious, were you? About being George Washington in my next book? Bob, let me tell you something. As a Sturdy Kid, you're great. But, as a Hero, let's face it, you bombed in Chapter Two."

"Bombed? I was *fantastic!*"

The Writer gritted his teeth. "We won't go into that now. Anyway, you just would not make a good George Washington."

"I bet I could do the bit about cutting down the tree!" exclaimed Bob. "Except I'd do it better. I'd blame it on someone else. That's what a real President would do."

"Enough!" snapped the Writer. "It's almost time for you to go back. If Martin goes outside and discovers you've left the Clubhouse, I'll have to change the story again."

Suddenly the Writer seemed very tired. "That's what I hate most about this business!

Everything has to be written over and over and over. When one thing changes, everything else has to change too or the story won't make sense. And if the story is nonsense, the Reader gets confused or, even worse, bored."

Bob yawned.

"Pay attention," snapped the Writer. "No one cares if *you're* bored! I'm the boss, do you hear me!" The Writer's voice echoed in the empty trash bin.

"Okay," said Bob reluctantly, "what's your problem?"

The Writer pointed to the page in his typewriter. "For one thing, it's this next Chapter. The one right after this. I've got a great ending, but no beginning."

Bob looked over the Writer's shoulder at the story. "What's the ending?"

The Writer smiled. "I know you'll love it, since you seem to dislike the Reader so much. You see, I'm going to work it so that by the end of the Chapter, he's hiding in a trash can, just like this one. As soon as the Reader thinks he's safe, the lid opens and a truck dumps—"

"I get it," shouted Bob. "That's fantastic! I'd love to be there and see his face. What Chapter did you say it was?"

The Writer glanced down at the paper. "Let's see. Chapter Five, it looks like."

A shudder went up Bob's spine. "Boss," he said quietly, "this *is* Chapter Five."

"What! That's impossible!" shouted the Writer. "It can't be!"

But it was, and the lid of the trash bin opened. And a truck dumped five hundred pounds of soggy garbage inside.

CHAPTER SIX

The Sturdy Kids and Martin were on a bus heading for the Deadwood Arms Hotel. Martin was worried. It was getting later and later in the day, and his hopes that the Sturdy Kids would be able to help him get back the belt were vanishing.

Mainly, it was their disguises. Spike and Becky were dressed as a king and queen, complete with ermine capes and golden crowns. Martin had been offered a crown to wear too, but he had refused. You couldn't sneak up on a stone dressed like that, especially when you came on a bus!

Bob was even worse. He wasn't wearing a costume, but from somewhere he had gotten a banana peel draped over his head and coffee grounds mixed up with his hair.

"The Sturdy Kids I remember never went around in disguises like this," muttered Martin bitterly. Their bus stopped in front of the hotel. "The Writer will see us coming for sure."

"That's where you're wrong," said Becky. "The Writer will be expecting us in normal disguises—dressed as bellboys or something. Now cheer up, and remember, you're supposed to be our son, Prince Basil."

Martin took a long look at Becky, whose crown was slipping over her right eye. Then he looked at Spike, who was forever tripping over his robe. Martin sighed.

At that moment, the hotel doors flew open. A tall, distinguished bell captain with gold braid on every part of his uniform hurried down the steps. When he reached Becky and Spike, he bowed deeply, almost to the sidewalk.

"Ah, Your Majesties," he said, "welcome to our humble hotel."

The bell captain led them all, even the bad-smelling Bob, up the stairs into a huge lobby. It was filled with antique furniture, and the walls were covered with paintings of famous kings and queens. On the floor lay a thick velvet rug, which sighed deeply with every step upon it. Overhead, a gigantic chandelier sparkled merrily.

"Do you suppose those are real diamonds?" Becky giggled as she pointed up at the chandelier.

"Not a chance." Spike laughed. "The Writer wouldn't know a diamond from a baseball field."

"Your Majesty, they are real indeed!" boomed a voice. Martin and Becky turned. The hotel manager was looking across a counter at them. He had a little wax mustache and a monocle in his right eye.

"What a pleasure it is to have you, Madame la Queen, and Monsieur le King," said the manager, rubbing his hands together. "And these are two little paupers you have brought, no?"

"No!"

"No?"

"No," repeated Becky. Pointing to Martin, she said, "This is our son, Prince Basil."

"I understand perfectly," said the manager. "It is just the other one who is a pauper then,

the one with the banana peel? A favorite book of mine, *The Prince and the*—"

"NO!" said Becky. "He is a guest of ours. This is Robert, the Earl of Trashberry."

"Well," said the manager in astonishment. "I am proud to meet you all."

Martin bowed.

At this, Becky elbowed him sharply in the ribs. "Princes don't bow to commoners," she whispered.

"Oh." Martin smiled at the manager. "Sorry I bowed."

Becky's sharp little elbow shot out again.

"Princes never say 'I'm sorry' either," she whispered.

"Got it," said Martin. Again came the elbow! "Hey, watch it!"

"Except to their mothers," added Becky with a smile.

Martin glared, realizing he was being made fun of.

The manager was plainly getting more and more confused. "What room would you like?" he said desperately.

"Room 1312," said Becky.

"Very well," said the manager. He gave Becky the key. "Boris will show you to the room. Boris!"

An eager-looking young man with thick

glasses ran over from across the lobby. "Yes, sir!" He looked at Martin. "May I carry your bags, please?"

"We don't have any bags," said Martin helplessly.

"That's perfectly fine, Prince Basil," said Boris. "We always keep some extras on hand just in case."

Boris took two large suitcases from a nearby closet, and led Martin and the others into an elevator. He pushed the button for the thirteenth floor. The elevator went up and opened. Boris led them down to Room 1312.

Boris opened the door and put the suitcases on little folding stands. Martin stretched, then strolled across the room to look out the window at the street below.

The moment Martin's back was turned, Bob winked at Boris.

"Is everything set up?" Bob whispered.

Boris nodded quickly. "I've had to make a few changes, but the basic plan is still on. Just make sure you Characters get him into Room 1313. You know what to do after that."

"Leave it to us," said Bob with a nasty grin.

"Very good!" said Boris loudly. "Enjoy your room, Your Majesties." He turned to go out.

"Just a moment," said Becky.

"Yes, Your Majesty?"

She pulled a pencil out of the inside pocket of her cape. "Maybe this will help you write better," she said slyly. "Thanks for showing us up."

Boris' eyes nearly bugged out. "Shh! The Reader will guess!" Boris turned and stormed out of the room, slamming the door.

Martin heard the slam and turned away from the window. "Wow! What got him so mad?"

Becky bit her lip. She wanted to warn Martin, but she knew the time wasn't right. Reluctantly, she reached again into her pocket and took out the key to Room 1313.

"Here, Martin," she said, "you go search the room. If the belt isn't there, maybe you'll find another clue. Sooner or later, we'll track the Writer down."

"Aren't you coming with me?" asked Martin. "You're the detectives. I don't know the first thing about searching."

"If you've read our books, you know our methods," said Spike. "First check for secret panels. Then look for loose bricks."

"Suppose there aren't any loose bricks?" protested Martin.

"Then check for tight ones! Who cares? Just go do it." As Spike was saying this, he half-pushed, half-led Martin out of the room and into the hallway.

"Good luck!" said Spike, and he closed the door behind Martin.

That left Martin alone in the hotel corridor. He didn't really like the idea of sneaking into a strange room and rummaging around. But then Martin remembered the Sturdy Kids did it all the time. He was learning that real life and books weren't exactly the same.

Room 1313 was right across the hallway. Martin tiptoed over and put the key in the lock. Just as he started to turn the key, he heard a sound come from behind. Martin quickly pulled out the key and spun around.

"Bob! What are you doing out of the room?" Bob and two hotel maids were standing in the hall.

"We got a call from downstairs," said Bob nervously. "Someone sent us a basket of fruit. The manager sent up these maids to help me carry it up."

"Two maids for one little basket?"

"Oh, it's not a little basket," stammered Bob. "I-It's a huge basket. A hundred pounds at least. See you later!" And he hurried toward the elevator, followed by the maids in their white uniforms.

A one-hundred-pound basket of fruit? thought Martin. He turned back toward the door and put the key in again. Then he stopped. *Wait a minute,* he thought. *There was something funny about one of those maids. She looked real mean, like someone I've read about–I mean, I am reading about.*

Martin ran back to Room 1312 and knocked on the door. "Becky! Spike!" There was no answer.

Martin threw open the door and charged in. The room was empty. On the little folding stands, the suitcases lay open. Inside them were the ermine robes and gold crowns.

"So *that's* where the 'maids' came from. The maid uniforms were in the suitcases all along. Wow, have I been double-crossed!"

Martin looked at the key in his hand. It was plain a trap had been set. But by whom? It could only be the Writer. And that meant Becky, Spike and Bob had *never* been on Martin's side. He threw the key angrily to the floor. "I'm getting out of here!"

Martin ran back into the hallway, just in time to see the door to Room 1313 open! Two men, wearing masks over their faces, were backing out. Both were carrying guns, and one had a canvas sack with part of a diamond bracelet dangling from it.

The one with the sack was talking to someone inside the room. "Now you folks just stay real quiet, and no one will get hurt."

At that moment the elevator doors opened, and a third robber bounded into the hallway. "Look what I got, Vince!" he shouted. "The diamond chandelier!"

Then the robber with the huge chandelier stopped dead in his tracks. "Vince. Look behind you. A witness!"

The robber with the canvas bag closed the door to Room 1313. Then he turned very slowly and looked at Martin. The robber's eyes were hidden, but he had a very evil smile.

"This isn't a witness, Lefty," said the man. "This is a hostage!"

CHAPTER SEVEN

And a hostage Martin was. Tucked under Vince's arm, like a long loaf of French bread, he wriggled and struggled, but without much chance of getting away. As far as Vince was concerned, Martin might as well have been another sack of jewels; he held them both as tight.

The robbers' escape had been carefully planned. Out the nearest window, onto a fire escape, and down thirteen flights of stairs. In no time at all, the three gangsters plus Martin were on the street with guns pointing every which way.

"Where'd you park the heap, Lefty?" barked Vince. "The cops are sure to show up any second."

Lefty slapped his forehead. "Gosh, Vince. I left it right here. I know I did. I said to myself, 'Lefty, don't you forget where the car is.' So I put it right by this red post here. . . ."

"Post!" screamed Vince. "That's a fire hydrant!" Vince looked down the street and pointed. "And that's our getaway car, being towed away by the traffic department!"

"Whew, that's a relief," said Lefty, wiping his brow.

"A relief! Our car's being hauled off to a garage and you're happy?"

"Sure, we were out of gas, too!"

"Look, Vince," said the third robber impatiently, "what are we going to do?"

Vince threw up his arms in despair. "Who knows!" he cried.

"I know!" shouted Martin. "Catch me!" Both he and the sack of jewels were falling rapidly toward the sidewalk.

Vince managed to scoop up Martin and the jewels before they smacked into the pavement. And at that moment, Vince had an idea.

"To the subway!" he ordered.

The robbers were off, running for the street corner and the subway entrance. They were just in time, for a squad car full of police officers had spotted them and was hot in pursuit.

The robbers stumbled down a flight of cement stairs leading to the subway station. Being hardened criminals, they naturally didn't pay a fare. Instead, when they came to the turnstiles, they simply jumped over them.

A subway train blasted its way down the tunnel. It came to a stop and opened its doors. The robbers crowded on.

For some strange reason, the sight of the armed men, one of whom was carrying a sack of jewels and an upside-down boy, upset the passengers already on the train. No sooner had the robbers gotten on the train, than everyone else decided to get off.

At that very moment, the police officers came bounding down the stairs. They were still trying to work their way through the mob of escaping passengers, when the train doors closed and the train pulled out of the station.

The robbers all sat down.

"I thought only Heroes had narrow escapes," said Lefty.

"Aw shaddup!" said Vince.

Martin looked up (he was still upside down) at the robber carrying him. "You're Vince, aren't you?"

"What if I am?" snarled Vince.

"Would you mind carrying me right side up so I can see what's happening?"

"That's only fair, Vince," said Lefty. "I mean, just ask yourself. 'Vince, how would you like to be carried head facing down all the—"

"I said *shaddup!*" shouted Vince. "You want to carry the kid, you go ahead." And Vince thrust Martin into Lefty's powerful grasp.

The subway train came to a stop, and the third robber jumped up. "Let's get off here. I got an idea."

They ran out of the train, up the subway stairs and out onto the street. There, right in front of them, was the largest used-car lot in the city. B. TAKIN'S SECOND HAND SPECIALS, said the sign overhead. NO REASONABLE OFFER REFUSED.

Mr. Takin, an extremely plump man wearing a bright red and white shirt, striped pants, and matching suspenders, strolled out of an office.

"Hello, boys!" he said eagerly. Then he pointed at the chandelier Lefty had stolen from the hotel. "Say, that's a real nice piece of glass."

"Glass!" groaned Lefty. He dropped the chandelier in disgust. "Darn Writer!" he muttered.

71

"Shaddup, Lefty!" snapped Vince. Then he turned to Mr. Takin. "Listen, old man, we're stealing one of your cars."

Mr. Takin rubbed his chin. "You come to the right place then, boys. At my prices, these cars *are* steals. Take this beauty now. Got a stick shift dual cam triple carb four on the floor brass on the dash—"

"Didn't you hear me?" said Vince. "We're really going to steal one of your cars!"

"'Deed you are, indeed," replied the cheerful old fellow. "I'm going to make you a special price—only seven thousand dollars, and that's half what I paid. Go ahead, you're robbing me blind, but I'm too old to know better. They call me the biggest sucker west of—"

"BLAM!" Vince shot his pistol in the air.

Mr. Takin blinked. Then he smiled. "I'd shoot off my gun, too, if I heard a price like that. Tell you what I'll do. I'll even throw in a free gallon of oil."

With that, Mr. Takin opened the back seat of the car he had been showing the robbers. He poured a huge bucket of smelly black oil all over the back seat. The robbers looked on, aghast.

Mr. Takin wiped off his hands and launched right back into his sales pitch. "Gotta hand it to you, boys, you really drive a hard bargain. Don't know how I'm gonna make ends meet, but that's my problem, not yours, so—"

The third robber grabbed Vince by the arm. "Pay the old fool before he gives us another free gallon! We've got to get out of here!"

Vince reluctantly paid the old gentleman seven thousand dollars in hard-stolen money. The three robbers piled into the car and started off, only to discover that it backfired every twenty feet or so, would not go over thirty miles an hour, and blew its own horn whenever the steering wheel was turned.

But, still, the car did run, and the robbers were halfway over the bridge leading out of the city when suddenly they heard the chuffing sound of a helicopter overhead.

A loudspeaker boomed out. "This is the police. Give up. We've got you covered with machine guns!"

Vince groaned. Then he pointed to a clump of trees by the river on the other side of the bridge. "We've got a chance if we can just make it that far."

They did, but only barely. While the helicopter opened fire with nearly every kind of gun imaginable, the car lurched and backfired its way across the bridge, finally careening off the side of the road. The car turned over once and rocked to a stop.

The robbers and Martin scrambled out of the wreck. Thanks to the trees, they were protected from any more shooting from the helicopter.

Vince made sure that everyone was all right, then led his band under the cover of the trees toward the river. When they reached the river, Vince waded out into a large cluster of cattails growing by the water's edge. Then he smiled.

"Just like I hoped," he said. "When I was sent up to the Big House two years ago, I had this planned for my escape. Never did escape, but it's still here."

Vince pulled back some of the cattails. There, rocking gently back and forth in the current, was a fully equipped aluminum boat with an outboard motor.

Several minutes later, the boat with its gangster crew was chugging upstream. Lefty scanned the skies with a pair of binoculars. But the helicopter seemed to have disappeared.

Suddenly Lefty shouted. "Vince! There's a police boat about a mile down the river. It's closing on us fast!"

Vince turned around and swore a mighty oath. "We'll have to run for it!"

"Impossible!" Lefty shouted back. "It must be tying thirty knots."

"You mean going thirty knots," said the third robber severely.

75

"So that's what it is," said Lefty. "You know, I've always wondered what it meant when books talked about 'knots'. 'Could they be square knots?' I asked myself and—"

Martin could no longer keep silent. During all this he had been the only one keeping track of where the boat was going.

"Look out! We're running aground!"

He was too late. A treacherous sandbar loomed ahead of the tiny craft. With a horrible, crunching, scraping sound, the boat plowed into the sand.

The robbers, Martin, and the jewels flew overboard. Lefty caught Martin, Vince got the jewels, and the third robber led the way to shore.

At last they managed to struggle out of the water and onto the bank. There they hid while the police circled around Lefty's wrecked boat. After a few minutes the police turned their boat around and headed back down river. They had given the robbers up for lost.

Lefty sighed and looked at the third robber. "Well, Roderick, what do you think we should do now?"

Martin jumped. "Roderick! Is your name Roderick?"

The third robber's eyes narrowed. "What's it to you?"

"It means I've just caught on!" shouted Martin. "You're Roderick Sturdy, father of the Sturdy Kids. You're just in disguise. In the end you arrest the robbers and save the day. That's the way it always happens. The whole thing is just another one of the Writer's crummy stories!"

Roderick Sturdy's face got bright red, just as it did in the books. Only this time, Mr. Sturdy was not angry with a criminal. "All right!" he said nastily. "If you think you're such a smart Reader that you can predict the outcome, we don't *need* you anymore!"

"Yeah," snarled Lefty. "We'll find some other Reader who'll really be surprised."

Lefty stood up and whistled. Four horses ran out from behind a clump of trees.

Vince looked at Martin and shook his head sadly. "So long, kid. We really could have had a good time. Next book, don't be so quick to guess the ending."

The robbers jumped on their horses and rode off. The fourth horse (which had been meant for Martin) galloped after them.

Martin slumped back to the ground.

"And now," he sighed, "what is going to happen?"

CHAPTER EIGHT

The robbers yipped and yelled with joy as their horses ran, plunging through the woods, jumping fallen logs, and scrambling up the sides of hills.

After a couple of miles, they reined up in the middle of a clearing. Roderick Sturdy waved his gray fedora hat triumphantly in the air.

"Free!" he shouted. "I'm free at last of the story. No more Readers to guess me out. Now I can do whatever I want!"

Lefty rubbed his chin thoughtfully. "Say, Rod, what exactly *are* we going to do? After all, we've always had a Reader before. And you know what the Writer says about Readers. 'If you're not being read, you'll soon be blue.'"

"Aw shaddup!" snapped Vince. "We still have the Reader's horse, don't we?"

The robbers looked back to see the beautiful black stallion that the Writer had just written in, especially for Martin to ride.

The horse was there, all right, but a second later, it wasn't. It didn't run away or anything —it simply vanished!

The robbers groaned in unison. There was no need to say a word. They knew very well that as soon as a Character has no purpose in a book, he disappears—evaporates completely from the story. Without Martin for a rider, the stallion had no reason to be in the Book anymore. And so it had gone.

"We've got to get the Reader back, and fast!" shouted Roderick. And so the robbers rode back to the riverbank, pinching themselves along the way to make sure *they* had not begun to disappear.

When they got to the bank, Martin was gone!

"Maybe the Writer got rid of *him* instead of us," suggested Vince hopefully.

"Don't count on it," said Lefty slowly, shaking his head. "I think we're all in for big trouble."

"No!" said Vince. "There's got to be a way out. Let's see. Maybe I could pretend to be the Reader, and then—"

"We'd never get away with it, Vince." Lefty sighed. "We've got to tell the Writer what happened."

Once more the robbers rode off, this time glumly toward the spot where they had arranged with the Writer to bring Martin.

As they rode, an amazing change came over the countryside. The grass disappeared, and sagebrush took its place. Cactus sprouted from nowhere, and the land wrinkled up into ravines and arroyos.

The robbers' clothing changed, too. Vince's pinstriped suit became a leather vest, a red and white checkered shirt, and buckskin chaps. Roderick Sturdy's gray fedora hat turned black and swelled up to ten-gallon size. And Lefty found he was wearing a sombrero and sandals.

Why? It was all because the Writer, working furiously in a nearby cabin, had decided to turn the story from a Gangster book into a Western. The Writer had heard Martin guess about Roderick Sturdy at the end of Chapter Seven. Now the Writer hoped to interest (and recapture) Martin with a different plot.

The Writer crouched over his old typewriter.

He poked at the keys with two fingers, like a beginner playing "Chopsticks" on a piano. A corncob pipe dangled from the Writer's lips, and the rest of him wore a prospector's outfit—dusty boots, grubby denim overalls, and a beat-up fedora hat.

According to the Writer's plan, the robbers were supposed to have brought Martin to the cabin to start off Chapter Eight. But something had gone wrong. Three pages had gone by, and the robbers *still* hadn't shown up. Until they came, the Writer would have to fill up the chapter as best he could.

The Sturdy Kids sat across the room, dressed as Indians, or at least in the way the Writer thought Indians dressed. The Writer knew very little about clothes, so he always tried to get out of describing them. (One of the few things the Writer *did* know about, however, was fedora hats. He used fedora hats at least once in every story.)

"Woo—woo," howled Becky, putting her hand over her mouth. "How's that for a war cry?"

"That's all wrong!" said the Writer crossly. "They go more like 'Wow—wow!' "

Becky laughed. "Oh, now I get it!" She jumped up and ran around the cabin shouting, "Wow! Oh, wow!"

"Very funny!" said the Writer. "A real Indian

wouldn't like to see you making fun of him that way."

"I'm not making fun of Indians," said Becky. "I'm making fun of *you!* Here you don't know a single true fact about Indians, but you keep on writing them into your stories anyway. What's worse, you've made *us* be the Indians. At least you could have made up some new Characters!"

"KNOCK! KNOCK! KNOCK!"

The Writer looked at the cabin door. Then he covered his typewriter with an old tin washbasin. "I bet that's the robbers now," he whispered. "Do you kids know what to do?"

Becky, Spike, and Bob nodded.

The cabin door opened slowly. Lefty, Vince, and Roderick Sturdy slunk in, hiding their heads.

The Writer pretended to be afraid and threw up his hands. "Don't shoot," he pleaded. "If you men spare our lives, I'll give you my map to the Lost Welchman's Mine."

Lefty tugged awkwardly at the yellow bandanna around his neck. "You don't need to say all that, Boss. I know that's what you planned for this chapter, but we've sort of got bad news. You tell him, Vince."

"Aw shaddup," mumbled Vince.

"Then I'll tell him," said Lefty. "The truth is, the Reader got away."

For a moment there was a silence.

The Writer's eyes slowly grew wider and wider; his face turned redder and redder; and his fists clenched tighter and tighter.

"He got away? You LOST the Reader? You're joking. Tell me you're joking!"

Vince scurried behind a chair. "Let me explain, Boss," he began.

"There are *no* explanations!" roared the Writer. "There are *no* excuses! I've told you, I've warned you, I've even *begged* you—never, never, NEVER leave the Reader alone! How could you *do* this to me?"

By this time, Vince was quivering and trying to hide in the fireplace. There were tears in his eyes as he said, "We didn't mean any harm. Do you want us to go look for him?"

"It's too late for that!" snapped the Writer. "You know the punishment. I'm going to write you bunglers out of the Book for good!"

"NO!" screamed the robbers together. "Anything but that, Boss. Give us one more chance."

"Don't waste your breath," said the Writer coldly. He uncovered his typewriter and sat down to write:

"A giant groundhog walked into the cabin. It stuffed the robbers into its pouch and carried them out the door. The robbers screamed and pleaded, but to no avail. A minute later the horrible beast crawled into its burrow. Neither it nor the robbers were ever seen or heard from again."

"There!" said the Writer proudly, when he had finished typing. "What do you think of that?"

Spike stared in horror out the cabin door as the tip of the huge groundhog's tail disappeared into the earth. "Wow!" said Spike slowly. "You really did wipe—I mean, write them out."

The Writer nodded smugly. "And let that be a warning to each of you kids. I'm in charge of this Book. You'd better listen to me, or you'll wind up as *they* did."

The Writer stood up and brushed off his hands. "Now let's see what we can do about the Reader. Somehow we've got to get him back into the Book."

Bob scratched his head. "I guess I don't understand. If you've still got the belt, why do you care where the Reader is? He can't get out of the Book anyhow."

"My dear little Hero," said the Writer nastily, "the belt is just *one* way out of the Book. There is another way, however, and that is—to be bored. If the Reader gets bored, the Book

stops dead in its tracks, and we stop with it. Now do you understand? We've got to keep the Reader *interested!*"

The Writer bit his fingernails and paced back and forth across the cabin floor. Then he snapped his fingers.

"Aha! A Nature story! That's what I'll do. Readers always like stories with animals in them. But I've got to make it seem real."

"How can you do that?" asked Spike. "You don't know anything about animals. Look at that giant groundhog you just wrote about. Real groundhogs don't have pouches."

"Well, they do in my Book!" said the Writer.

"That just proves what I was saying," Spike said. "When the Reader finds out you're making up your facts as you go along, he'll stop believing. And the next step after that is boredom!"

The Writer bit his lip. "I hate to admit it, but you're right. So there's only one thing for me to do. I'll look up my facts in another book! Martin won't stand a chance!"

With that, the Writer threw open a trunk and began tossing encyclopedia volumes all over the floor.

"Bob, look up 'Amazing Accounts About Alligators.' It should be listed under *A*. Spike, you check for Pheasant Physiology Facts. It'll be in the *F* volume. And Becky—"

The Writer paused and looked over his shoulder. "Darn it, where is she?" He looked under the washbasin. "Becky! This is no time for playing games. We've all got to work together. Becky? BECKY!!!"

But there was no answer, and there wouldn't be one either. Becky was by then a hundred yards away, running as fast as she could.

She had just one idea. Of the three Sturdy Kids, Becky alone had truly wanted to help Martin. Now that the Writer had explained about the belt and the other way out of the Book, Becky at last had a plan. But she had to find Martin before he got fooled again.

CHAPTER NINE

Martin had enjoyed Chapter Eight. He liked being alone to enjoy the Book without bumping into the Writer's clumsy Plot on every page.

After the Robbers had ridden off in anger, Martin had climbed a high, rocky hill overlooking the river. As he sat on a rock, waiting for his clothes to dry, he had watched hundreds of boats of all kinds and descriptions pass up and down the river.

The ships came from every land and every period of history: Chinese junks, gypsy freighters, men-of-war, submarines, catamarans, barques, icebreakers, and even dugout canoes. Each was bound for or coming back from one of the billions of stories inside the Electric Book. It was as if everything that had happened, was happening, or even might happen was going on before Martin's eyes.

But his clothes finally dried, and the afternoon sun dropped a little lower. Martin remembered how late he was, the worry his parents must be having, and the horrible lecture he would get from Mr. Gunderson.

Everyone had let him down. The Sturdy Kids, even Becky, had given him the slip in the Deadwood Arms. The Robbers had left him to splash by the side of the river. Martin felt helpless.

Then Martin thought of the Writer. *He* had been rotten from the start and was probably still hiding somewhere, planning one of his unbelievable stories.

Martin gritted his teeth. He would not give up. If the only way out of the Book was to go back to the City and search for the Writer, then that is what he would have to do.

Martin stood up. The bridge the Robbers had crossed when making their escape wasn't too far away. Half an hour's walk would get him there.

He had just begun to make his way down the hill when, out of the corner of his eye, Martin saw a gray shape spring from behind a clump of bushes. The shape dashed up the hill and bounded over the top.

It happened so fast that Martin had no idea what the animal was. All he had seen clearly was a gray tail. It might have even been a rabbit, except that it was much too big.

All of Martin's good intentions flew out the window. The Writer could wait; Martin had to learn what that gray thing was.

Martin raced back up the hill and looked over the top into the gully on the other side. He hoped that whatever it was he had seen, it had not kept running.

It hadn't. The animal stood out plainly. A little over two feet high at the shoulder, it had gray-brown fur, a long nose, and a wide, bushy tail. It looked like a sled dog, but wasn't. Martin knew its name immediately—*Canis lupus lycaon*, the North American Timber Wolf.

The Wolf was peering into a deep hole in the side of the gully. Martin crouched down so the Wolf wouldn't see him.

The hole was actually a den, lined with moss and dead leaves. As Martin watched, three small cubs crept out of the den, blinking their eyes in the sunlight. When the cubs saw their mother, they perked up and began crowding around her. The Wolf touched each cub with her nose as if to count them.

Then she did a very strange thing. She bent down her head and, with a heave, threw up on the ground!

Martin wasn't surprised a bit, however. A voice inside his head seemed to say, "This is how wolves feed their young until the cubs are old enough to chew. The food is half-digested and—"

"Wait a minute!" shouted Martin. "How come I know all these facts? Something strange is going on!"

The Wolf's ears jumped up at the sound of Martin's shout, and in a second she had herded her cubs deep into the den.

"Oh, well." Martin sighed. "At least I got to see her for a little while."

("Drat!" stormed the Writer, back in his cabin. "So much for facts! This time you'll get a wolf you *can't* scare away!")

Martin turned around to go back down the hill, when suddenly he heard a few rocks sliding behind him. And *he* had not knocked them loose!

Martin held his breath and looked over his shoulder. Climbing steadily up from the bottom of the gully was another wolf!

91

And this one, this one was a monster! It stood easily four feet high at the shoulder and had eyes that glowed like coals. Two cruel teeth, curved like sabers, hung over its lower jaw. The Wolf gave Martin a long, long look, then growled deeply and hungrily.

Up the hill it stalked, breathing slowly and powerfully, more like a tiger than a wolf. Its ears lay flat against its head, and pure hate burned in the brute's eyes.

Martin gulped and began sliding down the hill toward the river. Then a huge dark something swished overhead, blacking out the sun for a second. It landed a few feet in front of him and spun back up on its feet.

It was the Wolf again! It had jumped fifty feet in the air! Martin backed up and dodged behind a tree.

The Wolf sneered, lunged, and bit the tree in half!

Never had Martin seen anything like those teeth! A steel trap or a fossil dinosaur's mouth was the closest he could remember. Martin turned to run, but found he was facing a boulder twice as tall as he and three times as long. He was cut off, without a chance!

"Martin!"

Martin looked up. It was Becky, on top of the boulder, waving frantically.

"Martin," she shouted, "Throw a rock at the wolf."

"What good will that do?" screamed Martin helplessly.

"Just do it!"

Martin bent down and picked up the largest rock he could manage. Even if he hit the Wolf square, it couldn't help. But there was nothing else to do, so he heaved the rock.

The Wolf's eyes turned even redder with hate. It opened its mouth and shot out a jet of flame, melting the rock in midflight!

"See what it did!" howled Martin.

"Exactly," exclaimed Becky. "What kind of wolf breathes fire, jumps over mountains, and bites down trees?"

"An imagin—" Martin's eyes suddenly lit up. He turned around to face the Wolf again, which was just about to spring.

"Just a stupid, imaginary wolf dreamed up by the Writer, that's all you are. You're as bad as the Robbers. In fact, why don't you go bother them for a while?"

When the Wolf heard that, its eyes grew very wide. "Join the Robbers?" it muttered fearfully. "Never!" And with that, the Wolf turned tail and dashed back over the hill and out of sight.

Becky climbed off the boulder and joined

Martin. "I'm really surprised you believed in that silly excuse for a wolf for as long as you did, Martin. I thought everybody knew that real wolves aren't bloodthirsty, and that—"

"Yeah, well, I did know that sort of, but—anyhow! Why are you here? You've been in with the Writer all along!"

Becky shook her head. "I wasn't, really I wasn't. Oh, I know we ditched you at the hotel, but I didn't have any other choice. There was no way we could get the belt away from the Writer, unless we tricked him. So I had to pretend to go along with his plan."

Martin stared suspiciously at her. "I think it was a simple double-cross. And now you're trying it again. If you've got the belt, I just *might* believe you."

"But you don't need the belt"—Becky laughed —"that's what's so amazing. Just listen for a minute."

"Sorry," said Martin coldly. "I've listened to you before. And look where it got me! Stuck on a raft, chased by a shark, kidnapped, shot at, and now nearly chewed up by a phony wolf. Tell your story to some other Reader. I'm through!"

Becky grabbed Martin's arm. "That's the spirit! Try again!"

"Huh!" sputtered Martin.

She nearly danced around him. "I told you it was simple. The whole belt business was just a trick. You don't need it at all! Be bored, that's all. If you get bored with the Book, it stops automatically, and you'll be out. That's all there is to it!"

Martin thought for a moment. He looked at Becky's face carefully. She looked truthful. And what she said did make sense. A book should keep its reader interested. If a reader got bored, he stopped. Did an Electric Book work the same?

"Well," he said doubtfully, "I'll try it." Martin closed his eyes and wrinkled up his forehead.

A minute later he opened up his eyes. Martin put his hand to his mouth and stared fearfully at Becky. "I can't do it!" he cried. "I'm not bored. This Book has still got me!"

CHAPTER TEN

"How can I be bored?" Martin repeated. "I've been stuck three days in an Electric Book and can't get out. What's dull about that?"

"Can you even pretend to be bored?" Becky pleaded.

Martin frowned. "I could try, I suppose." He stretched his arms and forced a deep yawn. "Ho-hum! This Book sure is boring!"

"You can do better than that," said Becky. "Watch me. I'll show you how I acted in the *Case of the Two-by-four.* I was really bored in that book."

Becky walked to the side of the gully and sat down on a mossy stone. She folded her hands in her lap and sighed. Then she took the two ends of her braids and twisted them around each other. Finally, she stopped doing even that and just sat.

Martin whistled in admiration. "Hey, that *is* boring! Let me try again."

Martin picked up a small stone. He tossed it a few feet in the air and caught it on the way down. Then he did it again. And again.

After the third time Martin tossed the stone, Becky could no longer hold herself back. She jumped up, shouting, "Fantastic! That's amazingly boring. But do it harder. Think of something so boring it scares you. Think about geology!"

Martin's eyes lit up. "Geology? That's not boring at all! Look at this rock in my hand. I bet you didn't know it's over a million years old. It's made of three different chemicals: silicon—"

Becky clapped her hand over Martin's mouth. "Watch it!" she whispered. "You're getting interested again. That's how the Writer keeps you in the Book."

Martin nodded and went back to tossing his stone. Suddenly he shouted, "It's working! I can feel it. I *am* bored! This Book is boring,

boring, boring; I'm so bored that I could quit this very minute!"

And at that minute, the earth started to shake! Shocks raced through the ground in rhythmic beats, like the booms of a monstrous drum. Whomp! Whomp! Wham!

From somewhere up in the gully came a whirling mob of running people. Men and women of all ages, children, too. They stumbled and ran, ran and stumbled, doing their best to get away from something.

But what could be so horrible to start such a panic?

A passing man grabbed Martin's shoulder. "Run, you fools! It's King Komputer! He's broken his chains!"

The man pointed with a quivering finger up the gully in the direction from where he had come. Martin looked. "I don't see anything," he began to say.

And then he saw it.

A gigantic robot, fifty feet high at least, came lumbering down the gully. Each step the robot took boomed like a little earthquake.

WHOMP! WHOMP! WHOMP!

The robot's head spun around like the turret of a tank. Then a hole in the middle of the head opened. A laser ray shot out and melted a boulder down to slag in a second. The man

beside Martin turned and ran. "HOREEEG!" screamed a loudspeaker on the robot's chest.

Becky clutched Martin. "Remember. Pretend it's boring."

Martin gulped. "How can I? That's not boring!"

"WHHAAAAK!" screamed the Robot. With one of its crablike hands, the Robot plucked a tree up by the roots and tossed it over the side of the gully. "PAROOOG!" bellowed the Robot again.

"What it is," shouted Martin, "is unbelievable! I've never seen such a phony, boring plastic robot!"

Martin's words seemed to stun the mighty machine. Smoke poured out of its ears. "DO-WAAAAARN!" it groaned. Then sparks began to fly, and what had looked like a metal monster slowly melted down into a gray sticky pool of plastic. Only a silver windup key remained.

"Congratulations!" cried Becky. "Now we'll get the Writer for sure."

Before Martin could answer, the gully—stones, trees, and all—disappeared!

Suddenly he and Becky were standing in the middle of a flat, endless desert. The sun was no longer low in the sky, but now hung straight overhead, powerful and hot. No plants, no animals, no sign of anything could be seen around but sand and sand and sand.

Martin stared around wildly. They had no water, and he was already thirsty. What had happened? It didn't feel like a Chapter change. He looked at Becky. She was sitting peacefully on the sand as if nothing had happened at all.

"Oh, I see," said Martin slowly. "This is another trick of the Writer's, isn't it?"

Becky nodded.

Martin tilted his head back and shouted. "It won't work! I see through your tricks now. And they're still boring!" At that, Becky laughed with delight.

Then, from out of nowhere, a caravan appeared. Camel after camel walked by, each one loaded to the breaking point with heavy packages. Perched on the top of every camel's hump was a dusty man, wrapped from head to toe in white flowing robes. The very last rider pulled his camel to a stop beside Becky and Martin.

He had a long black mustache, hard, powerful eyes, and white teeth that flashed as he spoke.

"I am Sheik Azimir. This is my camel, Dagmud. It is not often we encounter strangers in the desert. Will you two be my guests until we reach the next oasis? I have many curious tales to relate, as I am sure you do also."

"No thanks," said Martin. "I've had enough stories. Yours would just bore me even more."

The Sheik's eyes narrowed. "Insolent dog!" He pulled a long and cruelly sharp scimitar from his belt. "Listen to my steel, then!" And he whirled the blade above him.

"He's bluffing!" snorted Becky.

"And how!" said Martin.

The sword seemed to give up and whirled lower and lower, like a helicopter running out of gas.

"Another time, maybe," said the Sheik in disgust. He put away the sword and reached for a sack tied to the side of his camel.

"Since you have shown such bravery, I give you this." And the Sheik untied the sack, taking out an old brass oil lamp. He threw the lamp at Martin's feet.

"Now, be off, Dagmud. We must rejoin the caravan!" The Sheik kicked his camel in the ribs. The camel flinched, then turned his head slowly around on his long neck. The camel appeared to be thinking. Then he puckered his lips and spit in the Sheik's eye!

Martin burst out laughing. That is, he laughed until Becky pinched him sharply. "But it served the Sheik right!" said Martin. Then he realized what Becky was trying to tell him.

"Oh, I see," said Martin. "The Writer set up

that joke, too." He looked at the camel severely. "That was very boring, Dagmud."

Dagmud glowered. Then the camel shrugged his shoulders, nearly throwing Sheik Azimir off. As the Sheik swore mighty oaths, Dagmud trotted off after the caravan.

Martin picked up the old tarnished lamp. "I've read enough stories to know what this is. It's just got to be another of the Writer's tricks."

"That's right," said Becky. "You'd better give it to me."

"Just let me hold it for a second," said Martin. "I'll still say that I'm bored."

Becky started to get nervous. She made a sudden grab for the lamp. "You'll ruin everything!" she shouted.

Martin barely managed to keep his hold on the lamp. "I know what I'm doing!" And the two of them tugged back and forth.

Suddenly the lamp began to shake! A cloud of swirling smoke poured up out of the spout. Gradually, the smoke began to form into a shape, the shape of a —

"Now see what you've done!" cried Becky. "You've gotten us into a whole new Chapter!"

CHAPTER ELEVEN

A Genie had appeared! He wore red and green silk robes and a turban that looked like too much bandage wrapped around the end of a thumb. From his towering height, the Genie gazed down on Becky and Martin. Slowly, he began to speak.

"Thousands of years ago, young master and mistress, I was a free spirit. Then came the day King Solomon decreed that I be imprisoned within the Lamp and—

"Skip all that," said Martin. "I've read it hundreds of times before. Just get to the part about the wishes."

The Genie's eyes drooped mournfully. "It's really very sad, you know," he said. "You Readers are all alike, these days. You only want to read the exciting parts. Personally, I think it's terrible. Excitement and adventure are like salt on food. Too much will spoil the—"

"The wishes!" shouted Martin. "I want my wishes!"

"Martin," said Becky, "you can't be taking this Genie seriously! The Writer will trap you again."

"Not this time. I've got an idea," said Martin. He turned to the Genie. "My wish is this. Take us out of the Book!"

The Genie rolled back his eyes until only the whites showed. Then his arms began to tremble like the branches of a tree in a storm. Then the Genie's whole body shook. And all at once he froze perfectly still! His eyes unrolled.

"Sorry. No can do."

Maritn roared. "Don't give me that! You're a Genie, aren't you?"

The Genie considered this. "True enough," he said at last. "If you had named a *place*, I would have had no trouble. The Hanging Gardens of Babylon, say. I could have you there in an instant. Or Twenty Thousand Leagues Under the Sea—that would be no trouble. I could even manage Mars. But out of the Book? Everything has to be in the Book, so how can I take you *out* of it?

"See?" said Becky. "I told you it wouldn't work. We should have stuck to the plan."

"Wait," said Martin, "I've got another idea. Genie, take us to the Writer!"

The Genie put his fingers to his lips nervously. "Are you sure you want to do that, young master?"

"I command you!"

The Genie nodded sadly. He clapped his hands softly and—

And a minute later the three of them were seated on a carpet flying swiftly over the pale yellow desert sands. The wind whistled in their ears, and Becky's braids flapped behind her head.

In less than a minute they had passed over the caravan and Sheik Azimir. The Sheik looked up and waved his scimitar in a friendly sort of way. Dagmud, however, was still in a sulk and barely even nodded.

As the caravan faded into the distance, Martin leaned toward the Genie. He had to shout to make himself heard over the wind. "How long till we find the Writer?"

107

"Sooner than you think," replied the Genie. Then the Genie pointed ahead. "Oh, oh. Look at that."

About a mile ahead, what seemed to be a huge brown wall had appeared. But it was much too high to be the wall of a city. No, it was not a wall—it was the edge of a swirling sandstorm!

"No way around it," shouted the Genie as the wind's roar turned into a howl. "We'll have to ride it out! Both of you, put on goggles to protect your eyes from the sand!"

"Where are we going to get goggles?" shouted Martin.

"Wish for them!"

"But that'll use up my third wish!"

"Tough luck!"

At that moment, they entered the storm. And it hit like a wall. It was like nothing Martin had ever felt, like a hundred or a thousand bees stinging at once. He covered his face, but it was no use—the sand was everywhere.

Through all this, the Genie chuckled merrily. On his face, a pair of handsome pilot goggles had sprouted as if by magic.

"Okay," shouted Martin at last, "I wish for two pairs of goggles. One for Becky and one for me."

The Genie snapped his fingers and instantly

a pair of goggles popped on Martin's head. He could see! Martin looked around at Becky. She too had goggles and was smiling happily.

But the sand should still be hurting my face, thought Martin. Then he realized. The sandstorm had stopped.

The Genie shoved his goggles back on his forehead. "Funny thing about these desert storms," he said slyly. "They stop as quick as they start. It's a shame you had to waste your last wish."

The carpet slowed down and began circling for a landing. It drifted lower and lower until finally it hovered about one foot above the ground.

"Well," said the Genie, counting on his stubby fingers, "three wishes made, three wishes kept."

"Wait a minute," protested Martin. "I didn't get my first wish, so it shouldn't count."

The Genie shrugged his shoulders. "It's not my fault your wish was impossible."

"But my second wish! To see the Writer. That's possible, but I never got it."

Becky broke in. "Oh, Martin, don't you see what he's done?"

The Genie smiled. "Listen to your friend, young master. Or should I say, young *Reader*? Don't you remember me?" The Genie slid his goggles back over his eyes. They looked very much like a pair of wire-rimmed glasses.

"You're the Writer!" shouted Martin.

"Bravo! I granted your wish before you made it. Now, I think I'll be going." The Writer tossed off his turban and stepped down from the rug. "Carpet, takes these two into Chapter Twel—"

"Geronimo!" shouted Martin as the carpet began to rise. He jumped and landed square on the Writer's back. The Writer grunted and collapsed to the sand.

"Becky!" called Martin. "Help me!"

"It's no use," cried Becky. "I'm just one of his Characters."

"No!" Martin shouted. "You're more than that!"

Martin felt the Writer gasping for breath. The man's wind had been knocked out, but in a few seconds it would be back. Martin had to have help!

"This is your last chance, Becky. You told me you wanted to be free from the Writer. If he gets away now, we'll never catch him."

The Writer gave a sudden heave and rose up on his hands and knees. Martin nearly lost his grip. He clung desperately around the man's neck. There was nothing else he could do.

"If you don't let go, kid"—the Writer panted

—"I'll put you through four hundred Chapters of fractions. You'lll never get out of this Book!"

Still Martin held on. Then the Writer reared back on his knees so that his hands were free. He grabbed Martin's fingers and began to twist.

One by one, Martin felt his fingers being pulled away. Then he was down to just two thumbs locked together. He was going to lose.

"Becky!"

And suddenly came a crash as Becky jumped on top of them from the carpet. The Writer toppled face-down in the sand.

In an instant Becky was up on her feet. "Grab his neck again, Martin. I'll get his legs!"

Like a cat, Becky pounced on the Writer's ankles. Then she slipped the goggles off her head and wrapped the elastic band around and around the man's legs.

"Quick, Martin, grab his hands."

While Martin held the Writer's arms behind his back, Becky used Martin's goggles to tie them together.

Becky stood back for a moment, panting. "Now for the belt," she said. She lifted the red and green robes, showing the blue denim overalls the Writer had worn in Chapter Eight.

In a second, she had unfastened the belt and was holding it out to Martin. "Here it is," she said. "Push the button, and you're out of the Book."

Martin slowly put on the belt. Suddenly, everything seemed unreal. He looked at Becky. "You're coming with me, aren't you? I mean, that was our plan. You wanted out of this Book."

Becky smiled and shook her head. "I can't go, Martin. There isn't any other book for me to go to. I have to stay here."

"I don't believe it," said Martin. "I'll talk to my parents. I have a sister at home. Maybe you could stay with her. We can do something!"

Becky smiled again. "I'd like that. But it's no use. You'd better be going now; the Writer will be getting loose soon."

"I don't care!" shouted Martin. "If you're not going, I won't go either." And he started to take off the belt.

"But you have to go," said Becky. "The Book is over." And she reached out and touched the red button in the middle of the silver buckle.

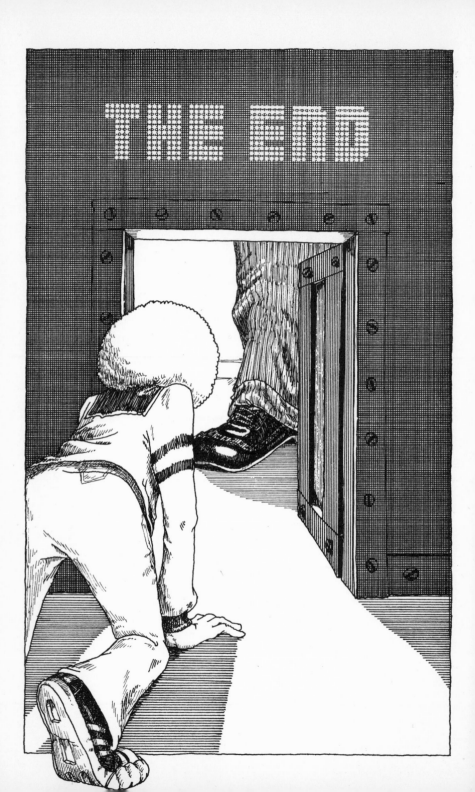

CHAPTER TWELVE

Red lights blinked in front of Martin's face; machinery hummed. For a moment, Martin was dazed. Then he realized—he was back in the machine!

Suddenly the lights gave a bright flash, spelling out the words: THE END. At the same time, there was a clicking noise and the door of the Electric Book slowly swung open.

Martin very cautiously looked outside. Could it be true that the Book was over? Or was this one last trick by the Writer?

Martin sighed with relief. He *was* in the laboratory again. Across the room, Mr. Jay was crouched over a typewriter, pushing buttons left and right.

"Mr. Jay!" shouted Martin. "I escaped!"

J.J. looked up from the typewriter and smiled. "I'm very glad to hear that, Martin," he said. Then he looked at his wristwatch. "You still have plenty of time before your bus leaves. You didn't have to hurry."

"Hurry!" Martin exclaimed. "I was stuck in the Book for three days!"

Mr. Jay beamed with delight when he heard that. "Actually, you've only been inside for half an hour. But I'm glad you thought the Book was so believable."

"Are you kidding?" gasped Martin. "I didn't believe a *word* of it. That's how I got out! But we can't talk now. There's a girl inside the Book named Becky. We've got to get her out before something horrible happens to her."

"Oh, I think Becky is safe from the Writer," said Mr. Jay. "And anyway—"

"Wait a minute," Martin interrupted. "How do you know about the Writer? I thought you hadn't read the Book."

"Well, uh, I," Mr. Jay stammered. "The truth is. . ."

But Martin had already guessed. He ducked

past Mr. Jay and ran to the typewriter. Sure enough, the last words that had been typed were THE END. And a thick electronic cable led from the back of the typewriter into the Electric Book.

Martin turned around slowly. "You're the real writer, aren't you, Mr. Jay? The Writer in the Book was just another one of your Characters, wasn't he? You made them all up, even Becky. Tell me the truth. She can *never* get out of the Book, can she?"

J.J. tugged nervously at his collar. "Well, after all, Martin, she *is* only a Character. The important thing is the story. And you liked that."

"I hated it! All you did was pull one corny trick after another, making up as you went along. And what a crummy ending! You just stopped, that's all. Whatever happened to Spike and Bob? You just forgot them after Chapter Eight."

Mr. Jay looked hurt. "What else could I do?" he protested. "I couldn't figure out how to work them back into the Plot."

"You couldn't figure out a *lot* of things!" shot back Martin. "Like that Robot. Was he corny!"

"He was supposed to be!" said J.J.

"But he was cornier than corny!" Martin stopped to catch his breath. Then he said,

"Look, Mr. Jay, read the Book for yourself. Then you'll know how horrible it is."

"I'll do that!" said Mr. Jay indignantly. "I'm sure it's not as bad as you say. And to prove it, I'll go through from the very start."

Mr. Jay leaned over the typewriter and pointed to a button. "Push this once I get inside. And don't touch anything else!"

Mr. Jay went over to the Electric Book. He waved proudly, stepped inside, and closed the door behind him.

And that is what Martin had been waiting for!

Martin sat down in front of the typewriter. He pushed the button to start the Electric Book. Then he did something else. He crossed out the words, THE END.

Then he took a deep breath and started to write.

CHAPTER THIRTEEN

"Chapter Thirteen!" exclaimed J.J. when the red lights flashed those words inside the machine. "I know I didn't write a Chapter Thirteen."

Then Mr. Jay slapped his forehead. "I bet that kid is monkeying around with the typewriter after all. I'd better get out of here right now!"

J.J. threw open the door of the Book and jumped outside. But he did not land in the laboratory.

Instead he found himself standing in the middle of a flat endless desert. The sun hung straight overhead, powerful and hot. No plants, no animals, no sign of—

Wait a minute! thought J.J. *I remember writing about this desert.*

"And do you remember writing about me?"

J.J. spun around in terror. "Who are you?" Then he relaxed slightly as he looked at the girl with braids and a wide smile. "You're Becky, aren't you?"

"Who else?" she said, still smiling. "This is where you left me, isn't it? In the middle of a desert at the end of a silly story!"

J.J. gulped. "Look, if you have any complaints about the way the Book ended, just tell me. I'll fix everything once I get out."

"And how do you plan to get out?" asked another voice.

J.J. jumped in fright. It was the Writer! And his hands were untied.

The Writer looked at J.J.'s stomach. "I notice you're not wearing your belt. That means the only way out is for you to get bored. And I have a funny feeling you're not going to be bored for a long time."

J.J. took a few steps backwards. "R-r-remember now. I wrote you Characters. This is *my* Book. I give the orders here. D-don't I?"

"Not any more," said Becky. "You're the Reader now. I think it's time for you to meet the rest of your characters."

"Oh, no!" pleaded J.J. "Suppose they didn't like what I wrote about them!"

"You'll find out what they think about your Book soon enough," said Becky.

Suddenly J.J. found himself surrounded. Everyone and everything seemed to be there. The Robbers, Bob and Spike, Mr. Takin, the entire Slug baseball team, the manager of the Deadwood Arms Hotel—even the wolves and the plastic robot!

The manager bowed. "What a pleasure to meet you at last, Mr. Jay."

"What-what are you going to do?" gasped J.J. fearfully.

The manager bowed again. "We are waiting for the one last character. He is coming now, I think. If you put your ear to the ground, you will know who I mean."

J.J. knelt down and listened. At first he heard nothing. Then there came the sound of something chewing, something tunneling rapidly through the earth.

"Not that!" screamed J.J. He jumped up and broke through the ring of characters, running as fast as he could across the desert.

A second later, the sand bulged up, and the huge head of the gigantic groundhog emerged.

"Tally ho!" shouted Becky. She jumped on the groundhog's back and led the characters in hot pursuit of Mr. Jay.

"What will we do when we catch him?" shouted Spike.

Becky looked down from her perch on top of the lumbering beast. "You'll find out soon enough in the next Chapter!" Then she laughed and laughed. "Tally ho! Tally ho!"

And Mr. Jay, followed by his characters, disappeared over the top of a large sand dune.

CHAPTER FOURTEEN

Martin stopped writing and turned off the typewriter. *That's enough for today,* he thought. *I have to plan out the next chapter carefully. Mr. Jay will get what he deserves, but I want the story to be worth reading too. Maybe I can even do something nice for Becky. . .*

Martin walked out of the laboratory, closing the door with its KEEP OUT sign behind him. As he walked down the hallway to rejoin his class, his mind was full of ideas for his story and for all the other stories he would write after that one.